LETTER TO AN UNKNOWN FRIEND

Children Promote Peace
between India and Pakistan

LETTER TO AN UNKNOWN FRIEND

Children Promote Peace
between India and Pakistan

Joseph Kalathil SJ

HENRY MARTYN INSTITUTE (HMI)
2018

Letter to an Unknown Friend: Children Promote Peace between India and Pakistan- jointly published by the Rev. Dr. Ashish Amos of the Indian Society for Promoting Christian Knowledge (ISPCK), Post Box 1585, Kashmere Gate, Delhi-110006 and Henry Martyn Institute (HMI), Shivarampally, Hyderabad-500052.

© HMI, 2018

ISBN: 978-81-8465-687-9

Cover design: Laura Ottaviani

Laser typeset by

ISPCK, Post Box 1585, 1654, Madarsa Road, Kashmere Gate, Delhi-110006 • *Tel:* 23866323

e-mail: ashish@ispck.org.in • ella@ispck.org.in
website: www.ispck.org.in

This little book is dedicated
to the children of our South Asian neighborhood …

May their future be blessed with peace and harmony …

*"When the power of love overcomes the love of power,
the world will know peace."* – **Jimi Hendrix**

Gratitude

We are deeply grateful to:
Honorable Shri Mani Shankar Aiyar for his Foreword …

Bishop Ignatius L. Mascarenhas and
Bishop Joseph Karikkassery, Fathers Thomas V. Kunnunkal SJ,
Michael Amaladoss SJ, George Fernandes SJ, Jerry Rosario SJ,
and Prof. Akhtarul Wasey for their Messages …

Rev. Dr. Samuel T. Packiam,
the Director of Henry Martyn Institute, Hyderabad, for his
generous contribution towards the printing of this book …

Laura Ottaviani for designing the cover pages …
and
Fr. George Pattery SJ, Provincial of the South Asian Jesuits,
for permission to print this book …

"Peace begins with a smile!" - **Mother Teresa**

Contents

Foreword

I am deeply touched to be invited by Father Joseph Kalathil SJ to write a foreword for his monograph on the remarkable mission he has been undertaking to promote peace between India and Pakistan. It is a mission in which I began to believe when I was sent as India's first ever Consul General to Karachi in 1978. We were received by the people of Karachi with astonishing warmth and generosity. Over the three years we spent in the country, our friendships extended beyond Karachi into the interior of Sindh and, through contacts made in Karachi and Islamabad, to all the provinces of the country. We were the recipients of affections and bonhomie from virtually every class of the society: the carpenters and painters and plumbers who worked on restoration of the many government of India properties in the city; the lakhs who thronged our visa office to find ways of meeting their long lost relatives in more than 300 districts of India; the elite who frequented the Sindh Club; businessmen from giant industrialists to small businesses; the tailor, the grocer, the sweeper who made our lives comfortable; even the Pakistani police posted around our home and our office to keep a beady eye on comings and goings of Pakistani visitors and check out on Pakistani friends who invited me to their homes; politicians of every hue, including the *Jamat-e-Islami* and *Jamiat Ulema-e-Pakistan* and ranging across the political spectrum to Bhutto's party, the PPP; a few Generals and many former army men; school teachers and college professors; and artists, musicians, painters and poetasters of every description; a few Hindus in the city but many in upper Sindh, particularly Jacobabad; and the wonderful Christians in the Convent of Jesus and Mary that my children attended. So bountiful was the love and respect we received that when our youngest daughter was born in Karachi, we called her Sana after learning that the name meant "the praise of god".

Through these years, the conviction grew in my mind that its only when we in India were to acknowledge and give due recognition to the vast peace community in Pakistan, the Pakistanis would also learn to acknowledge and recognize the huge constituencies of peace in India. We returned to India in early 1982 and over the last four decades, I reckon I must have visited Pakistan at least 40 times, occasionally on private, occasionally on government business, but most often at the invitation of think-tanks, schools and universities to talk to audiences, large and small, about the real possibilities of peace between the two countries, provided this is secure through "uninterrupted and uninterruptable" dialogue between the governments of two countries.

In Father Kalathil, I seem to have discovered a fellow-missionary, he in the name of God and I in the pursuit of my profession as diplomat and my vocation as a politician. Reading through the manuscript of this publication, I came across line after line that reflected my own thinking over the last 40 years and reverberated in my mind as I discovered the different paths by which Father Kalathil and I have arrived at similar conclusions.

In a message from Father Victor Edwin SJ, Director of the Delhi-based Vidyajyoti Centre for Christian-Muslim Relations, he suggests that what inspires Father Kalathil's work is "a certain apostolic aggressivity". That, I think , is the key to understanding what Father Kalathil has been doing with school children both in India and in Pakistan. While it was his Bishop, Ignatius Mascarenhas "who almost gave an order to me to take up the work of trying to build peace between India and Pakistan", he was left entirely to his own decision to try to find ways of doing so.

He initially confined himself to the minuscule Jesuit community, in the two countries and after securing a certain level of exposure to social and political realities in Pakistan went further to lay layer upon layer of different sections of society to harness them to his cause. While today, he justly takes joy in having spawned several peace groups such as Students for Peace, Teachers for Peace, Women for Peace, Lawyers for Peace, Writers for Peace, NGO's for Peace, Seminarians for Peace, Associations of People Praying for Peace and a soon to be formed Business People for Peace. In practical terms he began with school children of the two counties in the conviction that "Children normally are open minded and do not have strong prejudices".

The beginning of this exercise was simplicity itself. It began with his visiting three big catholic-run schools in Jammu and reaching out to three-thousand students, of whom about one percent, thirty-two students, agreed to give him "a letter each to an unknown friend in Pakistan." When he crossed the border and went to Pakistan, he initially found the response of Pakistani school children to be "rather negative". But by dint of perseverance, he ultimately succeeded in getting ninety-two letters from the Pakistani students of St Mary's School to "to an unknown Friend in India".

It is fascinating to read what the children learnt from this exercise of writing letters to unknown friends in the other country. Remarkably he has networked "over two thousand students from India and over the same number from Pakistan" and incorporated into his peace mission, thirty-five schools in Pakistan and thirty schools in India". The Pakistani schools stretch from Gujranwala to Faisalabad; and the ones in India from Jammu and Punjab to Jharkhand in the East and Bengaluru, Madurai and Kerala in the deep south. Moreover, beginning with catholic/church-run schools, the network now includes "Muslim-run schools, Sikh-run schools, other private schools and also Government schools".

Through this network, whose motto is " Peace is Possible" Father Kalathil is working on the mindset of the next generation in these two counties to internalize the dictums that "to live in peace is the right of every human person"; that "to live peacefully in India and Pakistan it is absolutely essential to have peace between the two countries"; that "it cannot be left to government alone to bring peace"; that, therefore, "this peace mission will have to expand to all sections of people"; and to accomplish the "gigantic task" of convincing people in both countries that peace between India and Pakistan "is indeed possible". There are marvelous tips on how to face up to difficulties and challenges, foremost among them being "my own prejudiced mindset and my dissidence; how to overcome bureaucratic and so-called national security hurdles in the two countries and how to get the children to speak to each other through letters that deal with everyday life". Father Kalathil says of the peace letters that he generated that some wrote about "the beauties and prosperity of their motherland"; some of their "varieties of dishes and cuisines"; some of "their appreciation for the dress of the friends across the border"; some "of famous monuments"; and yet others on "movies and songs from across the border". They also wrote about their studies; their own families and their desire to know about the culture of their new friends.

I commend this little monograph as an example of how one brave priest from a community that represents less than two percent of the population of India and Pakistan and hailing from a state far remote from the India-Pakistan border, has set a personal example that must be emulated by the statesmen and soldiers in whom the future of South Asia is lying. Obviously the challenges facing the government are far more complex than those being overcome by Father Kalathil's schools children, but governments, like school children and Father Kalathil himself need to "change my own mindset".

The Society of Jesus and children of all faiths who are found in both countries have shown the way forward. It is now for others to learn the significance of the Christian saying that "the truth often comes from the mouths of babes".

Mani Shankar Aiyar
G-43, Jangpura Extension
New Delhi-110014

Blessed are the peacemakers, for they will be called children of God
Introducing Father Joseph Kalathil SJ and his Peace Mission

F r. Joseph Kalathil comes from a generous, hardworking, God-fearing, religious family from Kerala. His father was a teacher and his mother a housewife. Both of them were very regular for the daily Holy Eucharist every morning and taught their children the primacy of God in their lives. He was the youngest in his family of eight children that included three cousins who lost their parents and were brought up by his parents. He was punctual at all the prayers and liturgical celebrations of the parish and was an altar boy and a pious member of the Sodality of Blessed Virgin Mary. He says: "My grandmother used to say constantly: 'Jose will study and will become a priest'. Thus, she inspired me to become a priest."

Fr. Kalathil's village is close to the southern bank of the ancient port of Kodungallore, where St. Thomas the Apostle is believed to have arrived in 52 C.E. The parish, known as St. Sebastian's Parish, had over 10,000 fervent Catholic members, with many vocations both for priesthood as well as for Religious Congregations. Many missionaries used to visit the parish and speak to young Catholic boys about the 'Missions' in view of getting some vocations for their religious congregations and mission dioceses. Some seeds of mission were sown in Joseph's heart by these missionaries.

Once the young Joseph happened to watch a volleyball match in which a team from Punjab was playing. He remembers that the tall, handsome players from Punjab were great at the game. He felt an urge to go to Punjab and work for Punjabis. The young Kalathil wrote to Monsignor Alban Swarbrick, the Prefect Apostolic of the Jalandhar Prefecture (in Punjab), and expressed his desire to be a missionary in Jalandhar. Monsignor Swarbrick welcomed him to Punjab but also alerted him to the many hardships, difficulties, obstacles and problems that he might face as a missionary there.

Kalathil completed his seminary formation in Lucknow and Allahabad and was ordained as a priest in 1969 and did fruitful ministry for many years in Punjab. The poor were always close to his heart. He wanted to help many cycle rickshaw drivers whom he knew. They worked hard but still did not own the rickshaws that they drove. He decided to give interest-free loans to them to buy rickshaws. This was a big moral boost for them. Their joy on becoming 'owners' of their rickshaw was tremendous.

Kalathil attended a 'Leadership Course of One Hundred Days' at Navjyoti Niketan, Patna, under a Jesuit, Fr. Edwin Daly. He met a number of Jesuits and felt a call to join the Jesuit order. As a Jesuit he has worked in many places in Bihar, Jharkhand and Punjab, for almost 30 years now. Everywhere he worked for the poor. Presently, Fr. Kalathil is the spiritual advisor to young seminarians at Kristu Jyoti Gururkul, Kauli in Punjab. Besides being a spiritual advisor for young people studying for religious service, he has been sowing seeds of peace in the hearts of young children in India as well as in Pakistan.

Kalathil is a peace activist who is busy, engaging in Peace Conversations with the children of India and Pakistan inspired by the teachings of Jesus: "Blessed are the peacemakers, for they will be called children of God" (Bible, Gospel of Matthew 5:9). He encourages children of these two nations to explore common elements between their cultures, religions, histories, arts, languages, and customs and recognise them as foundations for a peaceful neighborhood for all to live in harmony. Through exchanging letters of friendship and peace children themselves emerge as peacemakers. "Peace is possible" is his conviction. Kalathil further affirms that his conviction is based on his understanding of human person as we are created in the image and likeness of God, we all long for peace and we are oriented towards peace, since God is Peace.

Kalathil in his conversation with the present writer joyfully pointed out Pope Francis' teaching about living a reconciled life. Pope Francis in one of his homilies, reflecting on Matthew 5:20-26, invites us to live a reconciled life. The Pope says that Jesus desires 'radical reconciliation'. Reconciliation is not the same as good manners. It's a radical attitude, one that tries to respect the dignity of others as well as my own. From insult to reconciliation, from envy to friendship—this is the example that Jesus gives us today. Kalathil notes that both Pakistan and India, estranged neighbors, are in need of such radical reconciliation. I must say that I felt deeply inspired by his conviction and his courage to engage himself to work for Peace between these two neighbor-nations.

Kalathil continues to remain a source of encouragement to his Jesuit companions and others who work for peace. Father Kurian Emprayil SJ, the leader of the Jesuit community in which Father Kalathil lives, told this writer: "I am inspired by Kalathil's determination and passion for the Peace Mission. He enthuses and motivates young children to thirst for peace. When I interact with him, I am reminded of the words of the General Congregation 34, Decree 26 which states: 'We Jesuits and our colleagues are never content with the status quo, the known, the tried, the already existing. We are constantly driven to discover, redefine, and reach out for the magis. For us, frontiers and boundaries are not obstacles or ends, but new challenges to be faced, new opportunities to be welcomed. Indeed, ours is a holy boldness, a certain apostolic aggressivity, typical of our way of proceeding...'"

I am deeply grateful to Kalathil for spending time with

me, sharing about his life and peace mission in this interview. I hope this little booklet that carries some of his reflections on efforts to promote peace between people of India and Pakistan will inspire many others also to work for the same.

Joseph Victor Edwin SJ
Director
Vidyajyoti Centre for
Christian Muslim Relations
Vidyajyoti College of Theology
Delhi

October 22, *Feast of St. John Paul II*

Messages

Fr. Thomas V. Kunnunkal SJ
President, Islamic Studies Association
Delhi

*Connect what is presently disconnected
and thus redefine the impossible*

We live in a wonder world. Steven Kotler says in his book titled *The Rise of Superman* that more innovations, applications and conveniences have been made available to us in the last few decades than in the past 150,000 years of our human history. Science and technology, its executive engineer, are constantly redefining the impossible by making possible what most persons thought to be clearly impossible.

Making impossible possible is taking place not only in the field of science and technology but also in other fields of human enterprise. This happens when persons develop the courage of faith to break free of their fears: fear of failure, fear of ridicule, fear of criticism, namely, fear that the effort will be misunderstood, or wrong motives will be attributed. Fr. Joe Kalathil experienced these fears but anchored on his faith in God and believing in the goodness of persons, he found the courage to connect. We live in a sharply divided world. This is true of India and Pakistan. Who suffers from this disconnection? Both. Who gains? Neither. *Disconnection has become a growing epidemic globally and it has become the accepted pattern of behavior.*

Connect is a one-word action, a magical sesame key that will open new boundaries. True, connecting is often a difficult choice, and so we may be unwilling to connect. But once we develop the courage and connect, new vistas will open up and new relationships will result, bringing transformation in our homes, in our institutions and in the society at large. *This single wonder pill can cure the many ills of our world.* Peace will result on the basis of new relationships.

The invitation is *we take small steps to connect what is presently disconnected and thus redefine the impossible.*

Most Reverend Ignatius L. Mascarenhas
Bishop of Simla-Chandigarh

We sow seeds of peace

Late Bishop Peter Celestine and I initiated the Peace Mission to facilitate peace efforts between India and Pakistan. We invited Fr. Joe Kalathil SJ to explore ways for this mission ... the Lord was with him and the work progressed beyond our expectations. He chose children as Ambassadors of peace by facilitating the children of Pakistan and India to connect with one another. He obtained visa to visit Pakistan for this purpose several times. Peace is possible. Hostilities could cease as the seeds of peace is continually sown in the hearts and minds of people of both these nations. We sow seeds of peace and the God of history in His Providence and Wisdom will bring about Peace and Harmony among all people in this South Asian Neighborhood. I appreciate Fr. Joe Kalathil for his apostolic enthusiasm and gracious efforts for Peace.

Most Reverend Joseph Karikkassery
Bishop of Kottapuram
Kerala

May God bless all those
who strive for peace and harmony

I visited a number of schools in Pakistan. I am overjoyed to bring hundreds of very affectionate peace letters from those schools for the children of our schools in India. I am overwhelmed to find the Peace Mission initiated by Bishops Peter Celestine and Ignatius L. Mascarenhas bringing about fruits through the hard work of Fr. Joe Kalathil SJ. May God bless all those who strive for peace and harmony.

Prof. Akhtarul Wasey
President
Maulana Azad University, Jodhpur

May Allah bless all who work for peace and harmony

I am happy to know that Father Joseph Kalathil SJ through his contacts inspires and encourages many Indian as well as Pakistani children to reach out to one another in peace and friendship. I greatly admire his creative and courageous efforts in facilitating such cross boarder cultural contacts. Through his noble and timely efforts, Fr. Kalathil sows the seeds of peace and harmony in the hearts of several hundreds of children. As a result, children emerge as signs of peace and hope in the south Asian neighborhood. His efforts remind us that peace is possible and all of us should strive together to build peace and harmony. I am sure that this booklet, compiled by my friend Fr. Dr. Victor Edwin SJ, a noble soul and peace worker will warm the hearts of many to actively seek peace and understanding.

May Allah bless all who work for peace and harmony!

Fr. George Fernandes SJ
Provincial
Jamshedpur Jesuit Province

May Fr. Kalathil's work inspire many more persons
to be apostles of peace

I heartily appreciate Fr. Joseph Kalathil for his efforts on Indo-Pakistan Peace Mission, which is a very challenging work. At a time when peace and reconciliation is the need of the hour, the initiative taken by him has to gain momentum, if it has to have the desired effect. Initiating such difficult task is nothing new to Joe. He has pioneered quite a few challenging Missions in Jammu and Kashmir and Himachal Pradesh, such as Jammu-Kashmir Peace Mission, Kargil Mission, Lahaul–Spiti Mission, where he started a non-formal education programme in village Komik, which is considered to be the highest village of the world, situated in Spiti of Himachal Pradesh. However, publishing his interview about Indo-Pakistan Peace Mission during the Golden Jubilee Year of his Priesthood is a timely recognition of his indomitable, pioneering spirit. I wish him success in his every effort at promoting 'Peace' between the neighbors India and Pakistan. May the book inspire many more persons to be apostles of peace!

Fr. Jerry Rosario SJ

Theologian and Peace Activist

Chennai

All for God's greater glory - Al-ḥamdu lil-lāh

I commend the sincere efforts of Fr. Joe Kalathil SJ in working for peace between India and Pakistan through children. I had the privilege of visiting four dioceses and districts of Pakistan along with Fr. Kalathil during 15 to 29 of October, 2016 . Teaming up with him, I did participate in and contribute to 38 big and small Peace Schedules during that fortnight.

The Schedules included addressing / interacting / encountering / dialoguing ... with the inter-religious youth, ecumenical leaders, students, faculty members of educational institutions, major seminarians of philosophy and theology, women's forum, the MAGIS group, parishioners, animators and organizers of NGOs, candidates and formees, priests, religious women and men. There were also some families and individuals keenly interested and committed to the Indo-Pak Peace Mission who joined our conversations.

With the above experiential backdrop, let me say without any hesitation that this Peace Mission is the need of the hour. All the more, it becomes essential when the connectivity between India and Pakistan is currently at one of its lowest points.

Needless to add here what the 36th Jesuit General Congregation in 2016 had said in its clarion call regarding the focus of reconciliation and justice. The General Congregation had also released a Special Message of Solidarity to Ours in War Zones. In a broad sense, the Indo-Pak borders are also fall under that identity.

As a participant of and an eye-witness to its results and fruits so far, heartily do I wish to congratulate Father Joe Kalathil for this pioneering Ministry of Peace and Reconciliation in our JCSA zone. Fervently I do pray that this ministry, with all its required collaboration and cooperation, may bear more and more fruits of Shalom. All for God's Greater Glory! Al-ḥamdu lil-lāh!

1

Inspiration to Work for Peace

Where does your inspiration come from to work for peace between India and Pakistan?

In 1998, I was giving a retreat to the Congregation of the Sisters of Charity of Jesus and Mary community in Chogawa, a village in the Amritsar district in Punjab. Chogawa is about 10 kilometers from the border between India and Pakistan. While in Chogawa, Mr. Thomas, the music teacher of the convent school, invited me to his house. When I got there, a sad-looking elderly lady was sitting in the courtyard. Mr. Thomas introduced her to me, saying that she was his mother-in-law. I asked her name. Suddenly she became alive and joyful—someone was caring for her! She said her name was 'Shanti'. When I asked her from which village she was, she sadly pointed towards the border, meaning to say that she was originally from across the border, in what is now Pakistan. When I asked her who among her relatives still lived there, she said that she did not know since she could not get any news from across the border and if she made a phone call to her father or mother or to her brothers, the security people might harass her. Fearing this, she did not dare to make any contact with her near and dear ones living only about 25 kilometers away, across the border, in Pakistan.

I felt deeply hurt: what an inhuman situation! A woman is scared to contact even her own parents! Is it not a human-made awful situation? Can't human beings correct such an inhuman state of affairs? This was for me a decisive determination to work for helping people contact one another. It remained alive in me, though dormant due to unfavorable circumstances.

I think it was in the year 2000: The Superior General of the Society of Jesus[1], Father Peter-Hans Kolvenbach, visited Delhi when I talked about this to him and also gave to him in writing my interest in working for peace initiatives. Father General was very happy to hear about my plans and encouraged me to work on them. But even after talking to Father General and getting his approval I could not make a concrete plan with regard to peace initiatives since I could not generate support for the idea of peace between India and Pakistan from my Jesuit companions as peace was considered as something 'impossible' between the two countries. But it continued to be in my mind, though again, it remained dormant.

---

[1] Society of Jesus is a worldwide Catholic religious organization that runs educational, cultural and social service institutions. See: http://www.sjweb.info

In 2009, my Provincial[2] sent me to work in the Simla-Chandigarh diocese, under Bishop Ignatius Mascarenhas. In 2011, Bishop Peter Celestine of the Jammu-Srinagar diocese called me to Jammu for a meeting. When I went there, he asked me to start working on efforts to build peace between India and Pakistan. Although it was something I was interested in, when I was called to action I got a shock! In the shock, I declined the Bishop's request, giving several reasons why I could not do as he had suggested.

Bishop Peter Celestine then contacted Bishop Ignatius Mascarenhas, who almost gave an order to me to take up the work of trying to build peace between India and Pakistan, leaving no option for me to decline. I was completely lost and dejected: How to do this? Where to begin? Whom should I contact? How to go to Pakistan? Where in Pakistan to go and whom to meet—I did not know anyone there! And so on. Many more questions with no answers!

But then a ray of light emerged when my spirit being at the lowest! The very next day, the 'Tribune' newspaper published a picture of a young man, Gurmeet Singh Bajwa, a Sikh, who had finished his IT and MBA from Derbyshire University in the UK. Gurmeet Singh was offered very lucrative posts by several multinational companies. But he declined all of them, saying that he was going back to his village to help the villagers to come up in life. His village

---

[2] The Society of Jesus is organized into many units called 'provinces' for administrative reasons. The head of each unit is called a 'Provincial'.

was just along the international border between India and Pakistan, in the RS Pura area of Jammu district. It came to me as from the Lord: 'Here is the man. Work through him'.

Gurmeet Singh was very glad to help me to start work in the villages situated along the India-Pakistan border. The people with whom I work were very happy and gave me their full support. The work went very well for one year in the villages.

If there is to be peace between India and Pakistan, efforts have to be started in Pakistan also. So, in May 2012 I went to the Pakistan High Commission in New Delhi to request for a visa to visit Pakistan. They asked me if I had any relatives in Pakistan. I said: "No". They said that they would never give me a visa to visit Pakistan.

Though a bit disappointed I said: 'Lord, I did my job. The rest is up to You'. Believe it or not, by the end of September 2012 a visa was granted to me to visit Lahore for fifteen days! I have no other explanations for this except that the Lord's hand was active in and instrumental for my getting a visa to visit Pakistan.

From the very beginning of this work I could tangibly feel the active presence of the Lord. So, who was the inspiration? Mr. Thomas' mother-in-law Shanti, Father General Peter-Hans-Kolvenback, Bishop Peter Celestine, Bishop Ignatius Mascarenhas, Mr. Gurmeet Singh Bajwa, and the people of the villages along the Pak-India border in the RS Pura area. All of them had a share in giving me the 'inspiration'.

Certainly, the Lord himself used them all to help me and to inspire and encourage me to start and to sustain this work of the Lord.

2

Challenges in Peace Mission

*What were some of the initial difficulties
that came your way?*

The mission of bringing peace between India and Pakistan is the most challenging and most difficult mission I ever received during the past fifty years of my priestly life. Naturally, a great many difficulties and challenges came on the way. However, difficulties and challenges were not anything new to me since they were there in abundance from the very start of my priestly vocation.

Difficulties, challenges and problems help me to become aware of my own weaknesses and of the need for my dependence on the Lord. They make me work harder and give me much fulfillment. Thus, they help me to be more creative. They are opportunities to discover new ways of transforming challenges into success.

For me, success is not achieving what I want, but doing my duty to the best of my ability. Such an attitude has been instilled in me by my parents and teachers, for which I am grateful to them. Hence, I am always ready to 'fail' and also to make 'mistakes', because I strongly believe that only someone who does something will make a mistake. Therefore, I prefer to make a mistake and do something for Jesus than to escape from initiating something new, especially when it is something creative and challenging. The more challenging the job, the more satisfaction it gives me.

The first and foremost of the difficulties with regard to this work for peace between India and Pakistan that I faced was my own prejudiced mindset and my diffidence that I was not competent to undertake such a difficult and challenging mission, which I thought was too big for a small man like me. At this moment, the Lord stepped into action in a very tangible way to give assuring confidence to me, which helped me to overcome my diffidence and negative mindset. Another difficulty was the lack of support from Church circles. Although the mission was given to me by Bishop Peter Celestine and Bishop Ignatius Mascarenhas, none of the Catholic priests who work in the Jammu & Kashmir Diocese and the Simla-Chandigarh Diocese was ready to support me in this particular mission. In fact, there were people to oppose me and also to discourage those who were open to help me. Even one of the bishops of that region was against this mission. He clearly told me that he did not want me to start this peace mission in his diocese. However, all this did not discourage me. Many of the Catholic priests who belong to different religious congregations were afraid that they would get into trouble with the Government if they make any efforts in the line of peace between people of India and Pakistan, which they wanted to avoid at any cost. However, many lay people gave me support. With their support, the work progressed rather successfully. Here the saying came very true, that when one door is closed, the Lord will open ten new doors—which the Lord did!

Another difficulty the peace mission had to face was that of security agencies: the police, the CID, IB officers, and so on. They were after me in the initial stage, but I was not afraid of them. Fear is something that is not in me; for me, it is better to live one day without fear than go on living a thousand years with fear. I just cannot understand why people are afraid. As a child of God and as an Indian, I have my rights, for which I will not fight but will always stand up. Whenever the security people came to inquire about my visit to Pakistan, I took the stand: Honesty is the best policy. I am doing something noble, so why should I be afraid of anyone? Since I am doing the right thing, I have nothing to hide from anyone. The security people are doing their duty and let them do their duty well—that was my attitude. Thus, the difficulty of facing the security people was transformed into an opportunity to win them over for approving peace initiatives.

When I reached Lahore for the first time, in 2012, the Jesuit community of Lahore was very happy and said that it was the first time that an Indian Jesuit had visited the community. The head of the Jesuit community was Fr. Renato. He went out of his way to introduce me to different people, both Muslims and Christians. The people I met were all very happy about the mission, because everyone wants peace. However, the difficulty was to give hope to them. Really, they did not have any hope that there could be peace between India and Pakistan. Although these people were all happy and gave me full support and cooperation, their inner feelings were: 'People like this man come and will go back, never to return'.

Naturally, after I returned to India, absolutely nothing of a peace mission was done in Lahore for a year. When I visited Lahore the second time, in 2013, people whom I met gave me more support than they gave the first time. But again, after I returned, absolutely nothing was done in Pakistan about the peace mission, because people I met there had very little hope that something could be done effectively to bring peace between the two countries.

But when I went to Pakistan for the third time, in 2014, the hope of the people was strengthened, and they took the mission rather seriously. I read through them that they had begun to have some hope that peace is possible with India. Noticing this, I guided the friends whom I made in Pakistan to form different groups, like Lawyers for Peace, Women for

Peace, Youth for Peace, Teachers for Peace, and so on, and also a core committee to supervise, monitor and coordinate the activities of the groups. The core committee took the work seriously, and the work progressed.

Another difficulty was that the work of bringing peace between Pakistan and India being a very sensitive issue, precautions needed to be taken that it did not go into wrong hands. Hence, I limited my involvement only among Christians. Christians in Pakistan form only 1.8 % of the total population and their fear was that, being such a tiny minority, what could they do? They had to be reminded that as Christians they were the 'salt' of the earth and how in terms of quantity, a relatively little salt is enough to provide taste to the food. They also had to be reminded that the peace mission is the Lord's mission and that nothing is impossible for God. Being Christians, it was their duty to respond to the Lord generously, which they did. And the work progressed.

To convince Christian institutions, especially schools in India, to join the peace mission, was another challenge in the beginning. With much difficulty, three big schools of Jammu joined the peace mission since Bishop Peter Celestine, the Bishop of Jammu, supported it. When I visited a school in Pakistan, one of the senior students stood up and, pointing his finger at me, said: 'India is our enemy'. With a smile I asked if enemies were allowed to smile at each other. He responded positively. Then, I asked him, 'Can't enemies talk to each other?' He replied: 'They can'. So, I said: 'That is why

I am here!' We began to talk, and slowly enmity disappeared, and we became friends!

Another difficulty was that the visa one gets for Pakistan is limited. My visa allowed me to visit only three places, and one cannot go beyond what is permitted in the visa. So, wherever I could not reach I tried to make sure that the peace message reached there through some peace-loving, likeminded souls from Pakistan.

One thing is certain: The more challenging and difficult a mission is, the more help and support from God will come. When there is a compelling mission, taking ownership is an important issue. Although this peace mission has been given to me by two bishops, so far no one has taken the 'ownership' of it. Everyone highly appreciates this mission. But neither the official Catholic Church nor the Society of Jesus takes the ownership and responsibility for it. Apparently, it was discussed in the Regional Bishops' Conference, and the majority of the bishops were in favor of taking it as a work of the Regional Bishops' Conference, but just because one bishop raised an objection it was not accepted. So, very often I am being asked who is responsible for this peace mission.

However, in spite of such challenges and difficulties, the peace mission is making steady progress, because the Lord is active and his active hand can be felt in it.

3
Overcoming Challenges

How did you overcome the challenges you faced?

An effective way to overcome difficulties is to have a healthy attitude, which can help one to face the so-called 'difficulties' with faith in God and in oneself. Actually, there are no 'difficulties' as such. There are only events which are named as 'difficulties'. In reality, they are opportunities to abandon one's 'easy-chair comfort zones' to work to achieve success.

The first and foremost thing is not to get frightened of any so-called difficulty, however hard or huge it may seem to be. Face it with courage and look at it with deep faith in God as an event and have the strong conviction that nothing is impossible for God. What we call difficulties, problems or challenges are events which can be transformed into opportunities for achieving success, provided we face them with faith, courage and determination. So, what is needed is to have a positive mental frame. For example, when one of the Bishops did not want me to start the peace mission in his diocese, it was a good opportunity for me to understand his mindset and also a good opportunity to explore possibilities to reach out to other areas where the peace mission would be welcomed with enthusiasm. Similarly, when the security people came to inquire about my work, it was a good opportunity for me to make them too to realize that peace was the need of the hour and that it is indeed possible to build peace even between India and Pakistan and also to stand up for my right to promote peace.

Any difficulty or challenge can be transformed into an opportunity. All that we need is an open and fearless mind and firm determination.

When difficulties and challenges come, some people will get frightened and run away from them by trying to avoid them some way or other, but this is not a solution. One of the best ways to tackle difficulties and challenges is to face them with an open mind, a mind filled with faith, hope and a positive outlook. For taking such a course of action, one needs deep faith and trust in God as well as strong self-confidence. Self-confidence cannot be built up by theories or by just reading about it. It can be built only by doing what otherwise you would abandon as 'difficult'. I have been habituated with such practices of facing a challenging situation bravely rather than avoiding it or running away from it like a coward. Such a mental attitude is developed by life experiences. When we place our trust and confidence in God, he will surely help, and such help coming from the Lord will strengthen one's faith and one's confidence in oneself. This is what has happened in the case of our peace mission.

Some of the so-called difficulties will get solved by themselves in the course of time. All what is needed is to allow them to take their time, and time will solve them. So, we need to have patience and allow things to take their due course. For example, no one has taken the ownership of this peace mission. It does not worry me; I go on doing the work as far as I can, and the time will come when the Church leaders concerned will come forward to own it. Whenever I felt completely lost and helpless, God was always there to help me find the right solution. Our peace mission is God's mission, not mine, and he takes it ahead.

4

Children as Agents of Peace

Why did you choose to work with and through children to promote peace between India and Pakistan?

One principle on which the work of this peace mission started is: 'Begin small, begin with self, begin now'. Don't expect big things to happen. Don't pass on the responsibility for working for peace to others' shoulders—do it yourself. Do not postpone the work for tomorrow: tomorrow may never come.

Children are the best people to accept such simple principles. Promoting peace between India and Pakistan is literally tackling a seventy-year-old hostility, which is being promoted and perpetuated by powerful people for their own vested interests. Such a situation cannot be changed overnight. It will take time—maybe seventy years or even more—and we should be prepared for this. Hence, we need to set a long-time goal and impart peace education to the students of today. They can become agents of peace tomorrow to achieve this long-term goal. If we do not begin it now, peace will never come about between the two countries. Therefore, the urgent need is to do it *now*.

To build peace between the two hostile nations, one effective way is to connect people from both countries with each other. When they are connected, they start communicating with each other, which helps slowly to dissolve their prejudices and inhibitions *vis-à-vis* each other. The young, unprejudiced, open minds of students are best suited to begin such connections and communication, and schools are the best means to reach out to such young minds. Moreover, today's children are the leaders of tomorrow. If we train them today for peace-building, tomorrow they might be able to transform their society into a haven of peace.

One of the schools that takes a very active role in promoting peace is St. Anthony's High School, Lahore, where Mr. Nawaz Sharif, the former Prime Minister of Pakistan, and his brother, the present Chief Minister of the Pakistani Punjab, studied. The Principal of this school, Mr. Shahid Ambrose Moghul, gives full support to our peace mission. The students of such schools may become the leaders of tomorrow. If we train them today in peace-building, they might take this mission ahead, to transform their society into a haven of peace, and peace between India and Pakistan might also be a fruit of that.

Another reason for starting work with school children is that an effective way to influence an entire family is through children. When children are involved in a work or programme, their parents and other members of the family may also get involved.

Children normally are open-minded and do not have strong prejudices. Even if some prejudices are placed in their minds, they can be easily removed by exposing them to truth. A young mind is like wax, which can be moulded into whatever shape we want. It is very important to initiate children into such noble work as promoting peace, which is the need of the hour. It is also our responsibility to form them into peace-loving people.

5
Working with School Authorities

What were the initial responses from
the children and the authorities of the schools
to your efforts? Did they encourage you?

When this idea was put across to the students of three big Catholic-run schools in Jammu, it was not received well, because of the hostility towards Pakistan, which was being promoted among the people, including among the students. However, with repeated efforts, 32 students from out of over 3000 gave me a letter each to an unknown friend in Pakistan, which shows that overall, the students were not very enthusiastic about the whole idea. However, the idea of writing a letter to an unknown friend across the border was itself a fun thing, and children like to have some fun.

The response of the children in Pakistan was also rather negative in the beginning. When I addressed the first school, St. Mary's School in Lahore (run by the Apostolic Carmel

Sisters), there were over 600 senior students who attended the programme. This was in 2012. They gave me 92 letters.

But slowly, the mindset changed in a short time, and students in Pakistan began to respond positively. Also, in India, when the students received replies to the letters they had sent to Pakistan, they were all excited, and more students volunteered to be connected with students in Pakistan. Many even wanted to visit Pakistan.

It will take some more time to have exchange of students between India and Pakistan, for which we need to work on changing the mindset of the political leaders, which may also slowly happen. What we need is patience and perseverance.

The school authorities both in India and Pakistan had their fingers crossed; however, they did not oppose our efforts vehemently since one of the Indian bishops, the Bishop of Jammu-Kashmir, Bishop Peter Celestine, was supporting it. Sad to say, that the general attitude of the majority of teachers today is very narrow and is limited to the subject they deal with. They are basically concerned that the students should get a good grade in the subject they are teaching. Very few teachers look beyond their own subjects. At the same time though, there are some excellent people who understand what real education is and are ready to go out of their way to give the best of education to students. It is always a joy to meet them. Every time I meet such people, I get encouraged.

Two of such wonderful people who come to my mind are Mr. Harold Carver, Founder-Director of St. Stephen's

School, Chandigarh, and Mr. Roy da 'Silva, Principal of St. Stephen's School, Togan (Punjab). The work of the peace mission started and continues in Chandigarh only because of the magnanimity of Mr. Carver, who gave it his very encouraging and continuous support in spite of opposition from his own staff.

6
Letter to an Unknown Friend

How did the idea of Letter to an Unknown Friend come about? How do the children receive letters from unknown friends from across the border?

After I got a visa to visit Pakistan, I was totally lost and was disturbed: now I had no excuse not to go to Pakistan! Though I really wanted to visit Pakistan at least once, it was also a frightening wish, since I had received lot of negative information about Pakistan. But now no more did I have an excuse not to go to Pakistan. Whom to meet and how to begin the work of establishing peace between India and Pakistan? Who would support me in this work? Did the people of Pakistan want peace with India? A number of questions seemingly having no answer arose in my mind. What to do? How to do? Once again, I fell back to the Lord, placing all my trust and confidence in him and saying: 'Jesus, you gave me this mission, and now show me the way'.

After spending time in prayer and reflection I recalled a book I had read in the sixties, written by Raymond Pannikar. The title of the book was *The Unknown Christ of Hinduism*. The thought then came to me—why not write to an 'Unknown Friend of Pakistan'? Thus, the idea came about to connect students of India with students of Pakistan by encouraging them to write a 'Peace Letter' to an 'unknown friend' across the border. For some teachers, as well as students, this was 'stupid'! They laughed at me and asked me whom to address the letters to and what to write in the letters. Who would accept such a letter? It was not easy to make teachers and students understand the concept, nor was it easy to convince them of its usefulness. It was something un-heard of—writing a letter to an 'unknown friend', and, at the same time, it was a good joke for the students who heard about it for the first time! Finally, 32 students in Jammu gave me a letter each, addressed to an 'unknown friend'.

"Has not God made foolish the wisdom of the world?", the Bible (1 Cor. 1:20b) says, and this seems to be working here, too. Yes, the Lord's ways are mysterious. The teachers were also equally amused. It was not at all encouraging, but at the same time I did not find any other way of connecting students from India with students from Pakistan. So, out of sheer compulsion, I went ahead with the letter idea. Very often, one has to face such odd situations while launching something new and challenging; one needs to be branded as a 'fool' till success comes at the door!

Although initially students in Pakistan were not too enthusiastic to receive a letter addressed to an 'unknown friend of Pakistan', they were very happy to get letters from students in India and were excited beyond imagination when they received replies to their letters. With encouraging positive responses from students in both countries, the work progressed much better than expected.

7

Peace Letters

What are the main themes of these letters?

These are called peace letters or friendship letters. In these letters the students write only what can promote friendship and peace between the students. Many of the students wrote that they wanted peace between India and Pakistan. Some invited their counterpart across the border to join hands in order to promote peace. A good number expressed their desire to be friends and to communicate with each other. Some invited their friend to visit their country. Some wrote about the beauty and prosperity of their motherland. Some of them wrote about the varieties of dishes and cuisines in their country. Some expressed their appreciation for the dress of friends across the border. Some wrote about famous monuments in their country. Some of them wrote about different feasts that they celebrate. Some wrote that they liked movies and songs from across the border. Some wrote about their studies. Some wrote about their own families: what their parents were doing, how many brothers and sisters they had, and so on. A few also mentioned things of their culture and expressed the desire to know about the culture of their new friend. Almost all the students expressed their appreciation for the good things they had heard about their friend's country. A number of Pakistani students mentioned that they liked Hindi/Indian movies and dramas and TV programmes. Similarly, some of the Indian students expressed their appreciation for Pakistani songs. A few also highly appreciated Malala Yousafzai. Most expressed their desire to have peace between the two nations and stated that it is the duty of the young people of today to work for peace. Some of them also expressed their desire to visit and meet their relatives living across the border. A number of them wrote that some politicians foment conflict between the two countries and that there is an urgent need to come together to work for peace and development. Just a handful of the students wrote about religion.

In general, the letters written by the students to their unknown friends were a source of revelation to know the mindset of the students in both the countries. The letters encouraged me to strengthen my efforts to connect students across the border. It is very encouraging to know that some of the students still keep up their communication, through e-mail, Whatsapp and other such media.

Right now, there are 35 schools in Pakistan and 30 schools in India that have joined this programme. In India, about 10 schools are in Kerala, 2 schools in Madurai, one in Bangalore, three in Hyderabad, four in Chandigarh, one in

Mohali district-in Punjab, one in Sangrur, Punjab, two in Jammu, one in Odisha, and some in Jharkhand. In Pakistan, the schools are situated in Lahore, Gujranwala, Kasur and Faisalabad.

We began this programme with Catholic-run schools and slowly expanded into other schools. There are Muslim-run schools, Sikh-run schools, other private schools and also government schools in this programme. The majority of these schools are Church-run schools. So far, over 2000 students from India and over the same number from Pakistan has been contacted on the theme of peace and have written peace letters.

8

Children, Promoters
of Peace among Adults

How do you take the messages of these children
to the adult population?

The principle on which this peace mission started its work is to make the people of both the countries aware of the fact that:

(a) To live in peace is the right of every human person, and to secure this right, people will have to stand up for it and demand it.

(b) To live peacefully in India and in Pakistan it is absolutely essential to have peace between the two countries, which are presently being groomed as hostile to each other.

(c) It cannot be left to the governments alone to bring peace between the two countries. It is the right of every citizen to have peace, and the people should come together to build peace between the two countries.

When the people come together and demand their right to live in peace, the governments will have to concede their demands.

(d) Hence, this peace mission will have to expand its work into all sections of people in both the countries.

(e) For this, the first and foremost thing is to give hope to the people by convincing them that it is indeed possible to have peace between India and Pakistan, which is a gigantic task. Therefore, the motto 'Peace is Possible' on which we are working.

School students were only an initial point for beginning this gigantic but essential peace mission. How the peace mission could be taken into the 'adult' population was also a concern for us. We explored various ways and possibilities in this regard. Here, once again the Lord played his role and he proved the old saying true: 'When you take one step forward, the Lord will take you ten steps ahead'. Some students themselves got their parents, grandparents and others involved in their efforts to write letters to their 'unknown friends' across the border. Slowly, some of the teachers volunteered to write letters to teachers across the border. Perceiving the success of the children getting connected with students across the border, some lawyers came forward to form 'Lawyers for Peace'. Some formed 'Women for Peace'. Some youth came forward to form 'Youth for Peace'. These are all based in Lahore as personal initiatives.

In all of this, the Lord's active hand can be undoubtedly seen: for example, the case of how Bishop Joseph Karikasserry of Kottapuram Diocese in Kerala joined the peace mission. In January 2015 I happened to meet Bishop Joseph for the first time, in the Bishop's House in Kottapuram, in Trichoor district in Kerala. He asked me what I was doing in North India. I explained to him about working to promote peace between India and Pakistan. Immediately, he said that he also wanted to join the work and said: 'I will go to Pakistan with you'.

I took it as a joke but said that I was prepared to do whatever was needed for his going to Pakistan. After a week or so, I sent a message to the Bishop saying that if he was serious about going to Pakistan, he should give me a copy of his passport. It was a pleasant and a great surprise for me that he sent a copy of his passport through one of the officials of his diocese, who later tried his level best to dissuade the Bishop from going to Pakistan.

The news spread in the diocese that the Bishop was preparing to visit Pakistan. A good number of priests of his diocese pleaded with him not to visit that country. But the Bishop remained firm in his determination. Finally, the Bishop's office sent a message to me saying that the Bishop had given up his plan of visiting Pakistan. But since the Bishop had not contacted me, I went ahead with the work of getting a visa for him, and I asked the Bishop to send his passport to get a visa for him, which he did. Without even the Bishop going to Pakistan High Commission in New Delhi I got him a visa. The date was fixed to visit Pakistan as 2nd of October 2015. When this news spread, some priests, and even a Bishop from North India, tried their level best to persuade Bishop Joseph to abandon his plan of going to visit Pakistan, which he did not heed.

In a challenging mission like this peace mission we need to expect opposition, and blocks even from within our own circle, which has become a part of our normal life. Today, if we do not have any difficulty or opposition, we need to discern if we are doing the duty as the Lord wants us to do. Normally, such kind of opposition and difficulties are a sign of the vibrancy of a mission. So, what the Bishop faced not only did not bother us but even encouraged us to work harder. As for the question of how we faced all this, I have no other explanation for it except that it was the Lord's hand that made Bishop Karikasserry to take this decision and to stand firm on it.

Bishop Joseph had brought nearly 100 letters written by young Catholic children of his diocese addressed to the children of Pakistan. With this he started a new programme to pray for peace between India and Pakistan. Thus, was born what is known as 'Association of People Praying for Peace'. God's ways are mysterious. Consequently, today we have the following groups in Pakistan, and are also trying to have them in India:

(1) Students for Peace

(2) Teachers for Peace

(3) Women for Peace

(4) Lawyers for Peace

(5) Writers for Peace

(6) NGOs for Peace

(7) Seminarians for Peace

(8) Association of People Praying for Peace

(9) A core committee, to supervise and monitor the work of the peace mission, which has spread over to four dioceses of the Pakistani Punjab: Lahore Archdiocese, Faisalabad diocese, Multan diocese and Rawalpindi-Islamabad diocese.

Several Catholic Religious congregations are also involved in the work of the peace mission in Pakistan. At the proposal of the Archbishop of Lahore, the process has been initiated to form a new group: Business people for Peace. God willing, this new group will start functioning soon.

In all this, the active hand of the Lord has to be recognized. This peace mission is his mission, and he will take it forward. We only need to allow him to lead us.

When we called for a meeting of 'Women for Peace' for the first time, in Lahore, only six women attended: three Christians, and three Muslims. One of the three Muslim women was a medical doctor. After she returned, she called for a meeting of Women for Peace on the terrace of her house and invited me to address them. More than twenty-five women who participated in the meeting pledged their support to this peace mission. One of them was a member of the Punjab Assembly of Pakistan.

A young Muslim couple from Lahore heard about the peace mission and wanted to know more about it. The man is a businessman, and the lady is a professor in a university. They were very taken up by the peace mission and are now promoting it among their friends and associates. So, once again, you take one step forward and the Lord will take you ten steps ahead!

However, even with all what is given above, we cannot think of having achieved a lot. This peace mission is still in its infancy. We have many areas still to cover—like the spiritual sphere—and we have not even started to make use of the social media. And so on. At the same time, I am not in a hurry to get the work proceed very fast. The healthy growth of any good work requires a normal pace. Like India's freedom movement, which took 90 years (1857 to 1947), this peace mission also may take many decades of hard work. We still have to cover a very long distance.

I have a good number of people who help me in various ways for this mission. I should mention here Bishop Ignatius Loyola Mascarenhas, Bishop of Simla- Chandigarh, Bishop Joseph Karikkassery of Kottapuram Diocese, Archbishop

Felix Toppo, present Archbishop of Ranchi, Fr. Thomas V. Kunnunkal S.J., former Chairman of Central Board of Secondary Education, Fr. Victor Edwin, S.J., who is teaching Islam and Christian-Muslim Relations at Vidyajyoti College of Theology, Delhi, Fr. Lloyd S.J. of Bombay, Fr. Francis, S.J., Principal of St. Joseph's School, Kendrapada, Fr. Antony Raj S.J., the Principal of the College of Education, Jamshedpur, Fr. Kuruvila S.J., Principal of St. Xavier's School, Ghamaria; Mr. Harold Carver, Principal of St. Stephen's School, Chandigarh; Mr. Roy D'Silva, Principal of St. Stephen's School, Togan; Sr. Celia SCJM, and so on in India.

9

Peace is Possible

If peace between India and Pakistan is possible,
what are the measures you propose
to people of both countries?

First of all, the people of both countries should be convinced that it is possible to have peace between India and Pakistan. The governments of both the countries have their own agenda and they do have their important roles to play. However, left to the governments alone the possibility of having peace between the two countries is rather dim. Hence, building peace between India and Pakistan has to be essentially a 'people's movement', which slowly should spread into all sections of the citizens of both countries. As a people's movement we need to remember two dimensions of this movement: (1) one vertical dimension and (2) horizontal dimension.

The vertical dimension: From the very beginning of this peace mission, it has been perceived that it is a mission given by God through two Bishops: Bishop Peter Celestine and Bishop Ignatius Loyola Mascarenhas. God's tangible intervention has always been felt in this peace mission from its very beginning and every time it got stuck in its efforts to proceed ahead. In order to seek regular interventions and support from the Lord we need to form prayer groups in both countries, irrespective of the religious affiliation of the people supporting this work.

The horizontal dimension: If this peace mission has to be a 'people's movement', more and more people from every religious community and every social and cultural sphere should be brought into the mission and it has to be spread into every district and every town in both countries. It will take time—quite a number of years—and we need a lot of patience and must work hard at it, systematically and with open mind, welcoming anyone who wants to work for promoting peace. We need to place our trust and hope in the Lord, with the conviction that if today we do not take a step for bringing peace between the two countries, it may not happen for many years. Hence the need of acting today, even in a small way, beginning with oneself.

One of the questions people often ask is: Who 'owns' this peace mission? So far, no organization has taken the 'ownership' of the mission. It is very essential that some authentic organization accept this peace mission as its official mission. In 2015, when Bishop Joseph Karikasserry returned from Pakistan, he clearly mentioned that if the Society of Jesus (the Jesuits) officially takes it as the Society's mission, the peace mission can be very effective and one day, peace may prevail between the two countries. One of the reasons he gave for the Society of Jesus to take it up was that the peace mission will have to be 'owned' by an organization which is working in both countries under one leadership. Perhaps the Society of Jesus is the only Catholic organization which is functioning in both countries under the same leadership as that of the Jesuit Provincial of South Asia. Since the Jesuits have identified collaboration and networking to become a characteristic feature of the Society of Jesus in the years ahead, it is my prayerful dream that the Society of Jesus take this peace mission as its official mission. Once the Society of Jesus takes it up as its official mission, other Catholic Religious Congregations, like the Franciscans, Dominicans and so on, maybe happy to be partners in this mission.

Another prayerful dream of mine is: I am now almost 80 years old. It is high time that someone else takes up this mission.

Although this peace mission is still in its infancy, it is time to begin advocacy with different organizations as well as with the governments of the two countries. Media is another area which has to be more effectively used to promote peace between India and Pakistan.

When we work seriously, placing our trust and confidence in Jesus, more avenues of action will evolve. All that we need is to be open-minded to accept the new avenues as coming from the Lord.

Peace can be made by removing prejudices from the minds of people of both countries and instilling feelings of love and concern for each other. Love and concern for each other can be generated among the people of both the countries by connecting people with each other, thus forming a sort of relationship among them. This can very well be done by adults also through exchanging letters with each other.

We need the help of intellectuals. We can get their help and support by forming groups like 'Writers for Peace'. Also, by forming a network of 'NGOs for Peace' we can effectively reach a wider cross-section of society with the idea of peace.

10

Christian Commitment
to Peace Mission

*In working for peace between Pakistan and India
what things do you think one should keep in mind?*

Today's India and Pakistan were together as one country
under British rule. People belonging to different religions
and cultures lived together. Hindus and Muslims and Sikhs
and Christians came together to work for independence. It
is not any particular religious community alone that worked
for achieving independence. All people together worked as
one Indian people. Religion was misused to divide the one
united India into two nations. The seeds of hostility and
mutual enmity between Hindus and Muslims were sown
by some of the leaders for their own personal gain. What
happened after such hostility among the people was terrible:
two million people were killed, and sixteen million people
were displaced. Train loads of headless bodies of Muslims
were sent from India to Pakistan, and, similarly, train loads of
headless bodies of Sikhs and Hindus were sent from Pakistan

to India. Historians note it as one of the worst holocausts ever that had happened in the human history.

Groups of people used to catch strangers escaping across to the other side and the victims would have to prove that they belonged to the religion of the captors or else they would lose their head. If a group of Hindus catch a person, the victim has to prove that he or she is a Hindu to be let off; similarly, if a Muslim group caught a person, the victim would have to prove that he or she was a Muslim or else they were killed. The Christians were neutral, and neither Hindus nor Muslims would harm them. So, if the victims proved that they were Christians, the captors would let the victims free.

Hence, many escaping people, in order to save themselves, would wear a small cross round their neck to pass off as Christian. Thousands of people, though they were not Christians, saved themselves by wearing a cross round their necks. I have met many people who said that they saved themselves this way. The 'Cross of Christ' was literally the sign of salvation for many people at the time of the Partition.

Today, the Christian community is known as a peaceful community and Christians are known as peace-loving people. Hence, perhaps God, in his eternal plan, has designed that the 'peace-loving Christian people' should be the mediator for peace between India and Pakistan. From the part of the Church, one of the best gifts we can give to both India and Pakistan is to work for peace between the two countries.

www.ingramcontent.com/pod-product-compliance
Lightning Source LLC
Chambersburg PA
CBHW031720200626
46814CB00018B/1622